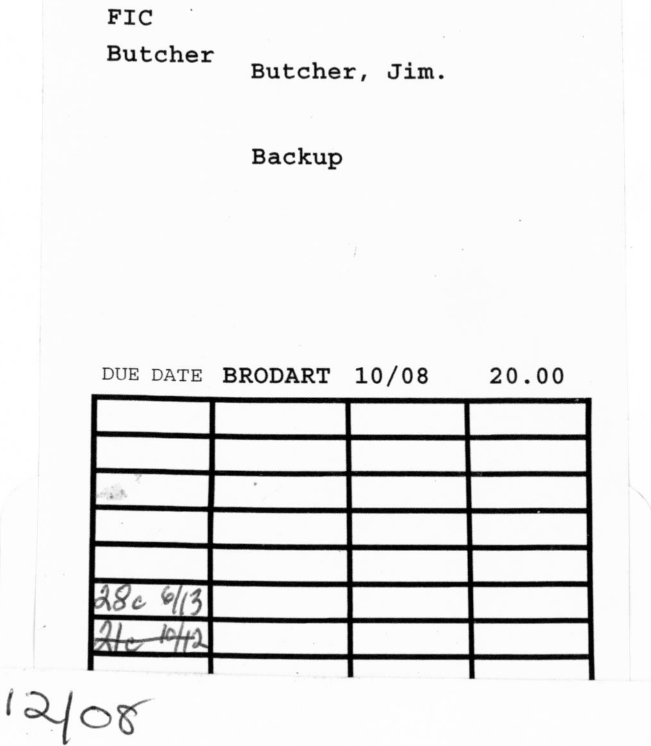

A Story of the Dresden Files

BACKUP

A Story of the Dresden Files

Jim Butcher

Subterranean Press 2008

First Edition

ISBN
978-1-59606-182-8

Subterranean Press
PO Box 190106
Burton, MI 48519

www.subterraneanpress.com

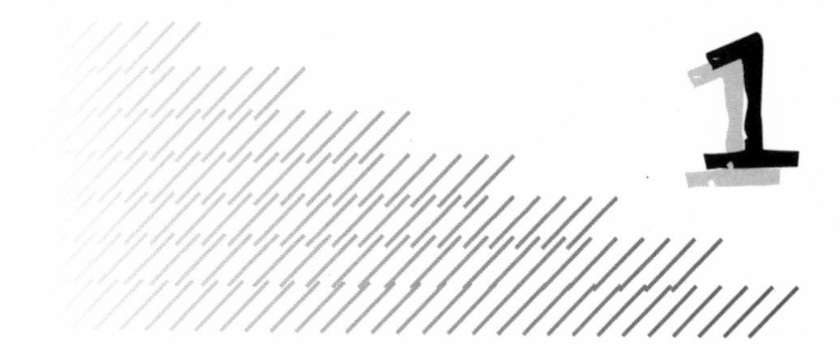

1

Let's get something clear right up front.

I'm not Harry Dresden.

Harry's a wizard. A genuine, honest-to-goodness wizard. He's Gandalf on crack and an IV of Red Bull, with a big leather coat and a .44 revolver in his pocket. He'll spit in the eye of gods and demons alike if he thinks it needs to be done, and to hell with the consequences—and yet somehow my little brother manages to remain a decent human being.

I'll be damned if I know how.

But then, I'll be damned regardless.

My name is Thomas Raith, and I'm a monster.

The computer in my little office clamored for my attention. I've got it set up to play Nazi Germany's national anthem whenever I receive email from someone in my family. Not my half-brother Harry, naturally. Harry and email go together like Robert Downey, Jr. and sobriety. I mean the other side of my family.

The monsters.

I finished cleaning off the work station and checked the clock. Five minutes until my next appointment. I took a quick look around my boutique, smiled at one of my regular customers, playfully scolded the young stylist working on her, and went back down the hall, around the corner, down the narrow stairwell and then through ten feet of claustrophobic hallway to get to my office. I sat down at the desk and nudged my laptop to life. The virus scanner pored over the email before it chimed again, a soft sound that a human wouldn't have heard from the end of the hall, much less from upstairs, and pronounced it safe.

The email from admin@whitecourt.com was empty, but the subject line read, "Re: 0b.11.v1.0n."

Oh.

Super.

Just what I needed.

I never really enjoyed hearing from that side of the family, even when the subject was something boring—like business pertaining to the war between the Vampire Courts and the wizards' White Council, for example. Whenever Lara wanted to get in touch with me, for any reason, it was bad news.

But when it was about an Oblivion matter, it was worse.

I had Lara's number on the speed-dial on my cell phone. I gave her a ring.

"Brother-mine," purred my eldest sister, her voice pure honey. It was the kind of voice that would give men ideas—really bad ideas, though they'd never realize that part. "You hardly ever call me anymore."

"I've hardly ever called you, Lara. Period." I ignored the lure she was sliding into her voice. She'd fed very recently—or was doing so at the moment. "What do you want?"

"You received my email?"

"Yes."

"There's a project I think you'll be interested in."

"Why?"

"Take a look at it," she said. "You'll understand."

The line was supposedly secure, but we both knew how much that was worth. Neither of us would mention any details over the phone—and we certainly would not use the word "oblivion." Too many Venatori had discovered, too late, that the enemy had very sharp ears, and that they would swiftly carry the war into the homes of those careless enough not to guard their tongues.

It had been nearly eight years since I had been involved in the Oblivion War. I suppose I had known that I couldn't avoid being drawn back into the fight forever. Lara, the only other Venator in the White Court, was largely occupied with her current responsibilities—namely, spending her days manipulating our father like a puppet on her psychic strings and ruling the White Court from the shadows behind his throne. Naturally, if something came up, she would pass it along to me to deal with.

"I'm busy," I told her.

"Grooming pets?" she said. "Trimming their fur? Checking for fleas? Priorities, brother-mine."

Lara is most annoying when she has a point. "Where do you want to meet?"

She laughed, a warm little sound. "Tommy, Tommy, I'm flattered that you want to be with me, but no. I've no time to spend playing games with you. I've sent a courier with everything you need and…Mmmmmm." Her voice turned into a sensual little purr of pleasure. "You know the stakes. Don't ask too many questions, brother-mine," she murmured. "Don't start using that pretty little head for anything taxing. Go back to your apartment. Talk to the courier. Take the job. Or you and I are going to have a very…ahhhhh…." Her breathing sped up. "A very serious falling out."

I could hear other soft sounds in the background, and another voice. A woman. Maybe two. Most of my family isn't what you'd call particular, when it comes to feeding on mortals.

"I'd tell you that you were a much nicer person before you got into the power-behind-the-throne game, Lara," I said. "But you were a bitch then, too."

I hung up on her before she had a chance to reply and went back upstairs, thinking. It was always good to get as much thinking done as you could, before the actual mind-boggling crisis came down. That way, when it got there and you only had half a second to decide what to do before something from beyond the borders of sanity started ripping at your soul, you could skip the preliminaries and go straight to the mistake.

When you deal with someone like my sister, you never take anything at face value. She was up to something. Whatever it was, it included putting pressure on me to hurry. Lara wanted me to rush into the situation blindly. If that's what she wanted me to do, it was probably a good idea not to do it.

Besides, I didn't want Lara to start getting used to the idea that I would run to do her bidding every time she snapped her fingers. More importantly, I didn't want to get into the habit of obeying her. It was an important first step toward becoming ensnared by more inflexible means, the way she had done to our father.

Anyway, I had a business to run.

And I was hungry.

Michelle Marion, eldest daughter of the Honorable Senator Marion of the Great State of

Illinois, had arrived a minute or two early for her haircut. My clients almost always did—especially the young ones. Michelle was a brunette, though you couldn't tell that by looking. Only her hairdresser knew for sure.

"Thomas!" she exclaimed, smiling at me, pronouncing it with the Latin emphasis. "What have you done with your hair?"

I had cut it a bit shorter after getting a rather large section of it burned off by a flaming arrow fired by a faerie assassin—but that isn't the sort of thing you share with your customers when you're supposed to be a flaming French master stylist. "Darling," I said, taking her hands and kissing her on either cheek.

The Hunger inside me stirred as my skin touched hers. The demon gleefully danced through her for a heartbeat or two, and as it did she shivered, her heart rate rose, and her pupils dilated. The Hunger told me what it always did about Michelle. Though she looked sweet, gentle, and kind, her repressed desires were far darker, and would make her easy prey. Fingers tightening in the back of her hair, feeling a man's body press hers against a wall—that was the stuff of her fantasies. She would follow me to the hall downstairs without hesitation. I could take her there. I could fulfill her desires, feed the Hunger, draw away her life and take my fill. I could leave my mark ripped into her mind and soul so that forever after she would come to me willingly, eagerly, yearning to be taken again and again and agai—

Until she died.

I pushed the Hunger back down into the corruption that passes for my soul, and smiled at Michelle, slipping on the accent as easily as an Italian leather glove. "I grew bored, so tediously bored, darling. I had half-decided to shave it all, just to shock everyone."

The girl laughed, her cheeks still flushed with excitement, in the wake of my demon's touch. "Don't you dare!"

"Have no fear," I assured her, tucking her arm through mine and walking her to my station. "The men who prefer such things aren't really my type in any case."

She laughed again, and I kept up the inane chatter until I could lean her chair back to the sink and begin washing her hair.

The Hunger lunged forward, eager as always—and I let it begin to feed upon the girl.

Michelle's eyes glazed over slightly as I went through the wash—very slowly, very thoroughly, working a full scalp massage into the process. I felt her mind slip into idle fantasy as the thin warmth of her aura pooled around my fingertips and slid up into me.

The Hunger screamed for me to do more, to take more, that it wasn't *enough*. But I didn't.

Feeding would have been…delicious. But it might have hurt her, too. It might even have killed her. So I kept on with the steady, gentle circular motions, barely tasting of her life force. She sighed in bliss as her fantasies dissolved into a gentle euphoria, and I shuddered with the need to give in to my Hunger and take more.

Some days, it was more difficult than others to hold back. But it's what I do. It's what I have left.

Michelle left about an hour later, hair trimmed, color retouched, blissfully relaxed, flushed, happy, and humming to herself under her breath. I watched her go, and my Hunger snarled and paced about restlessly in the cage I'd built for it in my thoughts, furious that the prey had escaped. For just a second, I found myself turning toward her, my weight shifting as if to take a step forward, to follow her to someplace quiet and—

I turned away and went back to my station, beginning the routine of cleaning. Not today. One day, doubtless, the Hunger would gain the upper hand again, and feed and feed until it was the only thing inside and there was nothing left of me.

But not today.

2

I left the store in the good hands of my employees and went out to my car, a white Hummer, huge, expensive, and ostentatious as hell. It was also one of the more robust vehicles a civilian could buy. Entire sections of houses could fall on it without causing it more than minor inconvenience, as could giant demon insects, and before you ask, I know it from experience. Just as I know that having a really tough vehicle on hand is not at all a bad move when you've made the kinds of enemies I have—which is to say, all of my own and pretty much all of my little brother's to boot.

Before I got in, I checked the engine, undercarriage, and interior for explosives. One reason Lara might have wanted me to hurry out might have been to make me rush out to the car, turn the ignition key, and blow tiny pieces of me all over Chicago.

I pulled up a mix list on the truck's MP3 player—Cole Porter and Mozart, mostly, with a dash of Violent Femmes—and headed back home to my apartment, hoping that whatever Lara had in mind for me, it wouldn't send me running to all corners of the earth. Again. Even though our breed of vampire doesn't share the others' weaknesses for sunlight and running water and so on, the kinds of places Oblivion missions had taken me hadn't exactly been tourist attractions.

I live in a trendy, expensive apartment building in Chicago's Gold Coast. It's not exactly to my taste, but it's the sort of place where Toe-moss the French stylist would live. One thing you learn young when you're a vampire is how to camouflage yourself, and to do that you have to sell every aspect of the disguise. It's a high-security building, but Lara's courier would be waiting for me in my apartment despite that. My sister had the resources to get it done.

Before I got out of the truck, I reached under the seat and slipped the sheathed kukri knife there into my coat, and tucked the barrel of my Desert Eagle into the waist of my leather pants, in back, hiding the grip under my coat. It had occurred to me, ten minutes into Michelle's appointment, that telling me to expect a courier in my apartment would be an excellent way to get me to lower my guard against an assassin who lurked inside, waiting for my return.

I went up to my apartment, took the knife in my teeth, and drew the gun, holding it low, the barrel parallel to my leg. Then I stood as far to the left of the door as I could, unlocked it, and pushed it open. No one opened fire. I waited for a moment more, just being quiet and listening, and picked out two things—the low throb of an excited heartbeat, and the scent of her shampoo.

Her shampoo.

I came through the door in a rush, discarding the weapons, and Justine met me on the other side. She threw her arms around me, and I had to fight to remember that if I didn't restrain my strength, I might hurt her as I hugged her back. She just pressed against me, everywhere, as if she wanted to just push herself inside me. She let out a soft little sob of laughter and pressed her face into my shirt.

She felt so good; soft and warm and alive.

We just stood there, holding one another for a long time.

My body surged with need, and an instant later, my Hunger howled in frenzied lust.

Justine. Our doe, our bottle of wine, ours, ours, ours. So many nights with her screaming under us, so many soft sighs, so many touches—so much rich, warm, madness-laced life rushing into us.

I ignored the demon—but while blocking it away, I moved my hand without really thinking about it, and stroked it over her hair.

Pain, pain so unreal, so unimaginably intense that I could not adequately describe it surged up my arm, as if the softness of those hairs had been the touch of high-power electrical cables. I hissed, my arm jerking away by pure reflex.

Sunlight, holy water, garlic and crosses don't bother an incubus of the White Court much. But the touch of someone who truly loves and is loved in return is a different story.

I glanced at my hand. It was already blistering.

Justine drew away from me, her lovely face distressed. "I'm sorry," she said. "I'm sorry, I didn't think."

I shook my head. "It's all right," I said quietly, and stepped back from her, while the demon screamed its frustration behind my eyes.

She bit her lip and looked up at me uncertainly.

It had been a long time since I had seen Justine face to face. I had forgotten how beautiful she was. The lines of her face had changed, subtly. She looked leaner now, more confident, more assured. Maybe I was too used to dealing with things that were immortal, or practically so. It's easy to forget how much difference a couple of years can make.

Her dark hair, of course, was gone now. It was growing in just as rich, long, and curling as before, but now it was silver-white. I'd done that to her—fed on her, drained her to the very edge of death, almost torn the life from her body in my eagerness to sate the Hunger.

I closed my eyes for a moment at the memory of that pleasure, and shivered. I'd nearly killed the woman I loved, and remembering it was nearly as arousing as her touch had been. When I opened my eyes again, Justine's gaze was steady and calm—and knowing.

"It doesn't make you a monster to want," she said, her voice very gentle. "It's what you do with the want that matters."

Instead of answering her, I turned and shut the door, then picked up my hardware. It isn't gentlemanly to leave weapons lying around on the floor. They clashed with the apartment's décor, too. I studied Justine from the corner of my eye as I did, taking in her clothing—elegant business-wear, suitable for Lara's executive assistant.

Or for a corporate courier.

"Empty night," I swore, viciously, suddenly furious.

Justine blinked at me. "What is it?"

"Lara," I spat. "What did she tell you?"

Justine shook her head slowly, frowning at me, as though trying to read my thoughts from my expression. "She said to bring you a briefing on a situation you needed to know about," she said. "Though for some reason, nothing could be written down. I had to memorize it all and bring it to you, along with some photos, here." She put a slender hand on a valise that sat on my coffee table.

I stared at her intently. Then I sat slowly down on one of the chairs in my apartment's living room. It wasn't a comfortable chair, but it was very, very expensive. "I need you to tell me everything she told you," I said. "Absolutely every word."

Justine stared back for a long moment, her frown deepening. "Why?"

Because *knowing* certain things, simply being *aware* of them, was dangerous. Because Justine had been providing me with information from within Lara's operation, and which I had, in turn, been providing to Harry, and through him to the White Council. If Lara had found out about that, she might have brought Justine into the Oblivion War. If she had, I was going to kill my sister.

"I need you to trust me, love," I said quietly. "But I can't tell you."

"But *why* can't you tell me?"

The real bitch about the Oblivion War was that question.

"Justine," I said, spreading my hands. "Please. Trust me."

Justine narrowed her eyes in wary thought, which took me somewhat aback. It was not an expression I was used to seeing on her face.

No. I was used to seeing a look of dazed satiation after I'd fed, or of molten desire as I stalked her, or of shattering ecstasy as I took her—

I closed my eyes, took a deep breath, and shoved my demon down again.

"My poor Thomas," she said quietly, when I opened them again. She sat down across the table from me, her dark eyes compassionate. "When we were together, I never realized how hard it was for you. Your demon is much stronger than theirs. Stronger than any but hers. Isn't it."

"It only matters if I give into it," I replied, more harshly than I meant to. "Which means it doesn't matter. Tell me, Justine. Please."

She folded her arms across her body, biting on her bottom lip. "It really isn't much. She said to tell you that word had come to her through the usual channels that the Ladies of the Dark River were in town." She opened the valise. "And that you would know which one you were dealing with." She took out a full-page photo, and slid it across the table to me. It was grainy, but big enough to clearly show an image of a stark-featured, young-looking woman getting into a cab at O'Hare. The time stamp on the photo said that it was from that morning.

"Yes," I said quietly. "I know her. I thought she was dead."

"Lara said that this person had taken a child," Justine continued. "Though she didn't say how she knew that. And that her aim was to draw out one who could do her cause great good."

I got a sick feeling in my stomach as Justine slid out the second photograph and pushed it across the table.

The photograph was simple, this time. A hallway, a picture of a door, its top half of frosted glass, bearing simple black lettering:

Harry Dresden, Wizard.

The door was closed, but I could see the outline of a tall, feminine form, facing an even taller, storkish, masculine outline.

The timestamp said that it was barely two hours before.

So.

Lara had been trying to do me a favor, after all. She had protected Justine behind a layer of generalities. And I had dithered around cutting hair and indulging my Hunger and my suspicions, while the Stygian Sisterhood had suckered my brother into a ploy to bring back one of their monstrous matrons.

Justine had never been stupid. Even when she'd been deep in my influence, before, she'd walked into it with her eyes open. "He's in trouble, isn't he?"

"And he doesn't even know it yet," I said quietly.

She pursed her lips in thought. "And you can't tell him why, can you? Any more than you could tell me."

I looked up at her helplessly.

"What are you going to do?" she asked.

I rose and reclaimed my knife and gun. "He's my brother," I said. "I'm going to cover his back."

"How are you going to explain it to him?" she asked.

I tugged on a pair of leather gloves and went to her, so that I could take her hands in mine, squeezing gently, before I turned to go.

"If he thinks he's helping her, and you interfere, he's not going to understand," she said. "How are you going to explain it to him, Thomas?"

It sucks to be a Venator.

"I'm not," I said quietly.

Then I and my demon went out to continue an ages-old silent war and help my brother.

I just hoped that the two activities wouldn't be mutually exclusive.

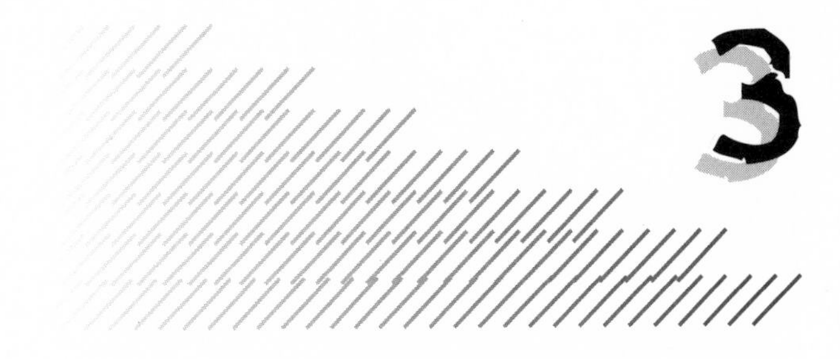

3

Justine had a driver circling the block, waiting for her to call. She did. I walked her to the elevator, holding her hand in my gloved fingers, the whole way. We didn't speak again. She smiled at me, though, when the elevator arrived, and kissed my fingers through the glove.

Then she was gone.

Technically, there was always a huge empty place inside me—that's what the Hunger was, after all.

So I told myself that this wasn't any different, and went back to my apartment to get to work.

Purely for form, I tried Harry's home and office phones before I left my apartment, but I got no answer at his apartment, and his answering service at his office. I left a message that I needed to talk to him, but doubted he would get it in time for it to be of any help. I grimaced as I took my cell phone out of my pocket and left it on my kitchen counter. There wasn't any point in carrying it with me. Technology doesn't get along well with magic. Twenty or thirty minutes in Harry's company could kill a cell phone if he was in a bad mood—less if he was actively throwing spells around.

My own remedial skills weren't any particular threat to the phone, but once I brought up the tracking spell I'd need to find my brother, my reception would go straight to hell anyway.

Harry waxes poetic about magic. He'll go on and on about how it comes from your feelings, and how it's a deep statement about the nature of your soul, and then he'll whip out some kind of half-divine, half-insane philosophy he's cobbled together from the words of saints and comic books about the importance of handling power responsibly. Get him rolling, and he'll go on and on and on.

For someone on Harry's level, maybe it's relevant. For the rest of us, here's what you need to know about magic: It's a skill. Anyone can learn it to one degree or another. Not very many people can be *good* at it. It takes a lot of practice and patience, it makes you tired, leaves you with headaches and muscle cramps, and everyone and their dog has an opinion about the "correct" way to do it.

Harry's a master of the skill—like, simultaneous doctorates from MIT, Harvard, Yale and Oxford master. By comparison, I went to a six-month vo-tech—which means that I skipped a bunch of the flowery crap and focused on learning some useful things that work.

It took me a couple of minutes longer than it would have taken him, but I used the silver pentacle amulet my mother had given me for my fifth birthday to create a link to Harry's amulet, a battered twin to mine.

Early springtime in Chicago can come at you with a psychotic array of weather. This spring had been pleasantly mild, and by the time I'd used the tracking spell to catch up to my little brother, the day had faded into a pleasantly brisk evening.

I held the silver amulet in my right hand, its chain wrapped around my knuckles, four or five inches above the pendant left dangling. The pendant swung steadily, back and forth in one direction, no matter which way I turned, as if it had been guided by a tiny gyroscope. I'd paid a small fortune to park the Hummer. Money well spent. Now I followed the swing of the pendant, and the spell guiding it, across the grounds of Millennium Park.

Millennium Park is something fairly rare—a genuinely beautiful park in the middle of a large city. Granted, the buildings spaced around the grounds look like something inspired by an Escher painting and a period of liberal chemical experimentation in an architect's underclassman years, but even they have their own kind of madman's charm. Even though night was coming on, the park was fairly busy. The skating rink stayed open until ten every night, and it would only stay open for a few more days before it would shut down until the seasons turned again. Kids and parents skated around the rink. Couples strolled together. Uniformed police officers patrolled in plain sight nearby, making sure that the good people of Chicago were kept safe from predators.

I spotted Harry stalking along the side of the skating rink, walking away from me. He was head and shoulders taller than most of the people around him, professional basketball-player tall, and rather foreboding in his big black duster. His head was down, his attention on something he was holding in his hands—probably a tracking spell of his own. I hurried across the distance to the skating rink to begin shadowing him.

I realized that I was being followed about twenty seconds later.

Whoever they were, the Stygian hadn't told them that they were dealing with a vampire. They hadn't stayed downwind, and a stray breeze had brought in the aromas of a couple of dozen humans who were nearby, the reek of a couple of trash cans, the scent of several nearby food vendors selling various temptations from their carts—and the distinct, rotten-meat and stale-sweat stench (badly hidden under generous splashes of Axe) of two ghouls.

That wasn't good. Like me, Ghouls can pass for human. They're the cheap muscle-for-hire of the supernatural world. Doubtless, the Stygian had hired them on against the possibility of interference from the Venatori.

One ghoul I could handle, no problem. Though they were tough to kill, strong, fast, and vicious as the day is long, that's nothing I haven't slaughtered before. Two of them, though, changed the picture. It meant that if they had any brains going for them at all, they could make it very difficult, if not impossible, for me to take them out without being incapacitated myself.

True, hired thugs generally weren't known for their brains, but it wasn't a good time to start making assumptions about the opposition. I quickened my pace, attempting to catch up with Harry, and pretended that I hadn't noticed the Ghouls.

Harry turned aside and hurried across the park grounds towards the Pavilion. It's an enormous structure, which I always thought looked something like a medieval Mongol's war helmet. Giant Atilla's chapeau, turned into a building, where concerts were held on a regular basis for the good people of Chicago. Tonight, though, the Pavilion was dark and empty. It should have been locked up—and probably was. Locks, though, never seemed to pose much of an obstacle to my brother. He went to a door on the side of the stage building of the Pavilion and opened it, vanishing inside.

I hurried after him, and called out his name. I was still a good fifty yards away, though, and he didn't hear me.

The ghouls did, though. I heard one of them snarl something to the other, and their footsteps quickened to a run.

I ran faster. I beat them to the door, and my demon and I shut it behind me, hard, hard enough to warp the metal door in its metal frame.

"Harry!" I shouted. "Harry, we need to talk!"

The ghouls hit the door and tried to open it. They didn't have much luck on the first try, but they settled in to wrench it open. The door was only metal. It wouldn't hold them out for long.

The interior of the building was empty and completely unlit, except for the faintest greenish radiance, which came through dimly, as though reflecting from many other interior surfaces, several rooms away. My demon had no trouble seeing through it, and I went through the halls in silent haste, following the faint light source toward its origin.

One of the ghouls ripped the door off its hinges, the metal shrieking behind me. One of the ghouls bounded through, snarling, the pitch and tenor of its voice changing as it came. It was changing form, growing less human and more dangerous as it ran down its prey.

I rounded a corner and ran toward a tall figure in a dark coat at the end of a hall, lit by a green luminescence—and realized within a few steps that the figure my tracking spell had taken me after was not my brother.

I drew the Desert Eagle from under my coat and opened fire. The form crouched, lifting an arm, and bullets bounced off of something and began skittering around the concrete of the hallway. A magical defense—the Stygian. A hand lifted, and a sphere of light flashed toward me. I dove under it, but the incoming spell matched my movement and fell to meet me.

There was a flash of brighter light, and an instant of heat that I expected to become agony. Instead, there was just a whirl of confusing dizziness, and then I was back on my feet—just as the first ghoul, its arms now half again as long as they were, and ending in grotesque claws, its face distended into a gaping, fanged muzzle, rounded the corner and leapt at me.

I'd brought the kukri. It's a weapon that's served the Ghurkas well for a couple of centuries, and with good reason. The bent-bladed knife, the size of a small sword, carries a tremendous amount of striking power along its inner edge when wielded properly, enough to strike limbs and heads from bodies, even when used by relatively small and less powerful mortals.

In the hands of a vampire, it's the kind of thing that jabberwocks get twitchy about.

The first ghoul led with a claw that was fast, but not fast enough. I left it on the floor of the hallway, hamstrung him on the back-stroke, and emptied the Desert Eagle into his back as he tried to flee, shattering his spine, one of the only ways to put a ghoul down fast and for keeps.

The second ghoul came at me a breath later, and hesitated for maybe a quarter of a second upon seeing what was left of the first ghoul. That isn't much in human terms. When you play in my league, the ghoul might as well have put a bullet through his own head. It would have been amounted to the same thing.

I threw the kukri, hard, my demon lending me strength and precision, and the knife split the ghoul's skull open like rotten fruit—the other way to put them down fast.

I slapped a new clip into the Desert Eagle and had it trained on the far end of the hall when the dark figure reappeared, lit by a faintly glowing green crystal she carried in her left hand. Her dark hair was tied back from her perfectly expressionless, motionless face, and her eyes were unreadably reptilian.

The Stygian.

"Balera, isn't it?" I asked her. The second ghoul's momentum had carried him to the ground beside me, and he lay there on his back, the handle of my knife sticking out of the center of his face, the interior of his skull open to view. One of his legs was still quivering. "Or are you Janera?"

"It matters little to us," she replied. Her voice was hollow, empty of something vital. It sounded about as much like a human voice as the old 60s electric pianos did like actual pianos. "You cannot win, Venator. The *Lexicon Malos will* be renewed. Depart now. Live to fight another day."

I leaned down and jerked my gore-soaked knife out of the dead ghoul. Then I started a steady, deliberate walk toward her. "That's what the other two members of the Stygian Sisterhood I've met have said. So far, it hasn't worked out that way." I started planning my shot. Every schmuck who can conjure up a shield that bounces bullets thinks he's hot stuff. But it takes concentration to do it, and the shields aren't omni-directional. A ricochet shot can bounce right around a conjured shield—and besides, if I could get her focused on the gun, she might not realize I was using the knife on her until it was too late.

There was a nice, smooth, polished metal surface behind her, the cover to what must have been a heating unit or a lighting control panel or something. The steel looked heavy enough to suit my purpose. If I could put part of a shot into her back, even just a few fragments from a shattered bullet, it should be distraction enough to let me put her down. "Let's make this simple," I told her. "Hold still, smile pretty, and your sisters can have an open-casket service."

Her lower lip twitched down away from her teeth in a gesture that looked like something that had never been human attempting a smile. "But yours," she said, her voice suddenly a purr, "will never know you."

I stepped forward, ready to shoot, and caught a flicker of my own reflection in the metal behind the Stygian.

It wasn't me.

The man facing me *wasn't me*.

He looked older, rough-faced, with shaggy graying hair and a scruff of a beard. His jaws were slightly distended, as were his lips, and I pegged him at once as a ghoul who had not quite managed to completely hide his true nature under a human outer appearance.

I lifted my left hand, and the knife in it, and the ghoul in the reflection did the same thing.

The Stygian gave me another not-smile and vanished around the corner.

It took me a second to recover and go running after her—but I needn't have bothered. A heavy door clanged shut as I rounded the corner, and flickering motes of greenish light danced over its surface before leaving me in total darkness. I'm not a member of the elite when it comes to the use of magic, but I knew better than to try to force that door against whatever energies the Stygian had lain across it in her wake.

I cursed savagely.

The entire affair had been an ambush and I had walked right into it.

This was the difference between Harry's use of magic and mine. The link between our amulets was strong enough that his more sophisticated spells would never have been deceived. The Stygian must have used some kind of masking enchantment to trick my own grade-school version of a tracking spell, and then employed an illusion to give herself the appearance of my brother once she had lured me into position to…do whatever it was she had done to me.

Why change my face? The Stygian Sisterhood were no amateurs when it came to dangerous, even lethal magic. Why had she done *that* instead of, for example, setting my intestines on fire? Even if my demon had been fully fed and at peak strength, I doubted I could have survived something like that.

Now that the actual fighting was over, I began to feel the fear. Had the Stygian wished it, I would be dead right now, and the knowledge was sobering, frightening. Harry had occasionally accused me of being reckless and overconfident—which is, believe me, hypocrisy of a staggering magnitude. But in this instance, he was probably right.

And after expending so much energy on running, fighting, and bending steel with my bare hands, I was *hungry*. The park outside this building was just brimming over with happy, oblivious kine. It would be so easy to cut one out of the herd, some tender little doe, and—

I had to focus and concentrate. I wasn't working with a safety net. Another stupid mistake could kill me.

"Get your game face on, Thomas," I snarled to myself. "Get your head together."

The darkness of the building was almost complete, but my demon let me see clearly enough. The ghouls were already rotting away. They'd be nothing but a stinking mess of sludge in a few hours. We were far enough into the building that I doubt the sound of the shots had carried out of it—but the cops on patrol in the park would notice the door the ghouls had torn off the building, probably sooner rather than later. I couldn't stay there.

I found another way out of the building and hurried back toward my truck. I couldn't trust my tracking spell, obviously, which meant that I had to find Harry another way. Karrin Murphy of Chicago

PD might be able to find out if anyone had seen his car, but I had no way of knowing Harry would be in it, or even nearby. And even if I *did* find him, it was going to be hell convincing him of anything when a stranger walked up, told Harry that he was his brother, and asked him to abandon a case.

First things first, I decided. I had to find him, or none of the rest of it would matter.

I knew someone who could help.

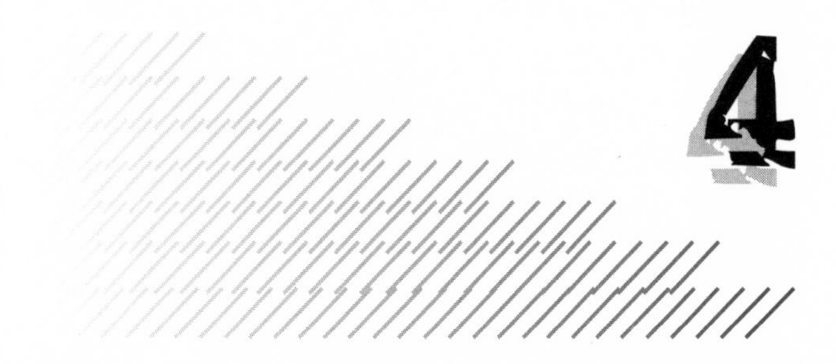

4

Harry is one of the top wizards on the planet and he lives in a basement.

His boarding house is a little run-down, but roomy. I guess the rent is cheap. His basement apartment is tiny, but the neighbors are elderly and quiet. He seems to like it. I've known him for years, and I still can't quite believe that he really keeps on living there.

Personally, I think that's why he hasn't had more trouble at home—I don't think his enemies can bring themselves to believe it, either. Maybe they figure it's a decoy he's constructed solely to give them somewhere obvious to attack, where he can lure them to their deaths. Certainly, the ones who show up don't like the welcome they receive. The defensive spells around his home could charbroil a herd of charging buffalo.

I used the crystal he'd given me to disarm his wards, and the key he'd given me to unlock his door and let myself in. His apartment was spotlessly clean, as usual—he'd turned into a neat freak a few years ago, for some reason, though he'd never talked about why.

An enormous, shaggy gray dog, two hundred pounds of muscle and fur and white, sharp fangs, appeared from the little kitchen-equipped alcove and growled at me.

"Whoah," I said, holding up my hands. "Mouse, it's me. Thomas."

Mouse's growl cut off suddenly. His ears twitched back and forth, and he tilted his head one way and then the other, peering at me, his nose twitching as he sniffed.

"Someone laid an illusion over me," I said. Harry had told me that his dog was special, and could understand human speech. I still wasn't sure whether or not he'd been pulling my leg when he said it. He's got a weird sense of humor, sometimes. But speaking quietly to animals when they appear nervous is always a good idea, and I did *not* want Mouse deciding that I was a threat. He was a Foo dog, and I'd seen him take on things no mortal animal could survive, much less overcome. "Look, boy, I think Harry might be in trouble. I need to talk to the skull."

Mouse came over to me and sniffed at me carefully. Then he made a chuffing sound, padded over to one of the throw rugs on the apartment's floor, and dragged it to one side, revealing the lift-up trap door that led down to the sub-basement.

I paced over to it and ruffled the dog's ears. "Thanks, boy."

Mouse wagged his tail at me.

A folding stepladder led down into my brother's laboratory, which I always pronounced with five syllables, just to give him a hard time. I unfolded it and went down, stopping as soon as I could see the whole place.

You don't just wander around a wizard's lab. It's a bad idea.

The place was piled high with god only knows what kind of horribly disturbing, rare, expensive, and inane junk. There was a lead box on one shelf in which he kept dust made from depleted uranium, for crying out loud. There was also an eight-foot-long scale model of the heart of the Chicago skyline on a table in the center of the room. It's obsessively detailed, down to models of trees that actually *look* like the trees they represent, and one of the downtown buildings that was recently demolished.

It's a little bit creepy, actually. My brother's got a voodoo doll of the entire *town*.

He also has a human skull that sits on its own wooden shelf, between a pair of candles that have been burned down and replaced so many times that little volcano-lumps of colored wax have formed at

either end. There are romance paperbacks stacked up on either side of the skull, along with an old issue of Playboy from the 70s, with Bo Derek on the cover, and a long strip of scarlet ribbon.

"Hey," I said. "Skull. Bob, isn't it?"

The skull didn't move.

I was going to feel really stupid if it turned out that Harry had been pulling my leg about the skull the whole time. My brother, the ventriloquist. "Hey," I said. "Skull. Look, it's me, Thomas. I know I don't look like Thomas, but it's me. Harry's in trouble, and I need your help to go get him out of it."

There was a tiny flicker of orange lights in one of the eye sockets of the skull. Then the flicker grew brighter, and was joined by a second in the other socket. The skull twitched on the shelf, turning a little toward me, and said, "Holy Clayface, Batman. What happened to you?"

I chewed on my bottom lip for a second, debating on what to tell the skull. I knew that Bob was Harry's lab assistant and technical advisor in matters magical, that he was some sort of spirit who resided inside the skull, and not a mortal being in his own right. All the same, he was beholden to Harry, and whatever Bob knew, Harry could potentially learn.

"There isn't much I can tell you," I said. "Harry's new client isn't what she appears to be. I was trying to warn him. She tricked me into following her and did this to my face. I think she did it to make it harder for me to warn Harry about her."

"Uh huh," Bob said. "What do you want from me?"

"Help me get this thing off my face. Then help me find Harry so I can get him off this case before he gets hurt."

Bob snorted. "Yeah, right."

I frowned. "What? You think I'm lying to you?"

"Look, Thomas," the skull said, its tone patently patronizing. "I acknowledge that you're cool beyond cool. You're good-looking, you get all the girls, and you send naked chicks to Harry's apartment dressed only in bits of red ribbon, all of which I admire in a person—but, uh. You're still kind of a vampire. From a house of vampires famous for being mindbenders, no less."

I ground my teeth. "You think someone's controlled me into doing this?"

"I think that generally speaking, you don't have secrets from your brother, man," Bob said, yawning. "And besides, once Harry gets onto a case for a client, he doesn't come off it. He's like a tick, only his head doesn't come off quite as easy, and there's less chance of him giving you an infection."

"This is important, Bob," I told him.

"So is finding lost children," Bob said. "Or at least it is to Harry. I thought it might be because then their mother would be all appreciative and jump into bed with him, but apparently it's one of those morality things. Finding kids hits some kind of good-versus-evil hot button in his head."

That's what Lara had meant when she said the Stygian had taken a child. Crap. Now I could see the Stygian Sisterhood's plan.

And if I didn't stop them—stop Harry—the Oblivion War could be lost in a night.

"Dammit," I growled. "Bob, I need the help. I need you to do this."

"Sorry, chief," Bob said. "Don't work for you. Harry tells me different, that's a different story."

"But he's in *trouble*," I said.

"So you say. But you aren't offering me any details, which makes it sound fishy."

"Because if I gave you any details, they might get back to Harry, and he might be in even more trouble than he is right now."

Bob stared at me for a second. Then he said, "I hereby promote you from mackerel to tuna fish."

"Okay," I said, thinking. Bob was a spirit. Such beings were bound by their words and promises, by the contracts they made with mortals. "Okay, look. You serve Harry, right?"

"Yep."

"If I give you this information," I said, "and if in your judgment his possession of this information could prove detrimental to his well-being, I want you to swear to me that you will keep it from him or anyone else who asks you about it."

"Okay," Bob said, drawing out the word with tremendous skepticism.

"If you do that," I said, "I'll tell you. If you can't, I won't. And bad things are going to happen."

The skull's eyelights brightened with what looked surprisingly like curiosity. "Okay, okay. I'll bite. You have a bargain. I do so swear it to you, vampire."

I took a deep breath, and glanced around. If another Venator knew what I was doing, they'd put a bullet in my head without thinking twice.

"Have you ever heard of the Oblivion War?"

"No," the skull said, promptly.

"For a reason," I said. "Because it's a war being waged for the memory of mankind."

"Uh," Bob said. "What?"

I sighed and brushed my gloved hand back over my hair. "Look. You know that for the most part, the old gods have grown less powerful over the years, or have changed as they were incorporated into other beliefs."

"Sure," Bob said. "Hasn't been a First Church of Marduk for a while now. But Tiamat got an illustration in the Monster Manual and had that role in that cartoon, so she's probably better off."

"Uh, okay," I said. "I'm not sure exactly what you're talking about, but generally speaking, you're right. Beings like Tiamat needed a certain amount of mortal belief to connect them to the mortal world."

The eyelights brightened. "Ah!" the skull said. "I get it! If no one *remembers* some has-been god, there's no connection left! It can't remain in the mortal world!"

"Right," I said quietly. "And we're not just talking about pagan gods. We're talking about things that people of today have no words for, no concept to adequately define. Demons of such appetites and fury that the only way mortals in some parts of the world survived them at *all* was with the help of some of those early gods. Demons who had to be stopped, permanently."

"You can't destroy a primal spiritual entity," Bob mused. "Even if you disperse it, it will just reform in time."

"But you can forget them," I said. "Shut them away. Leave them forever lost, outside the mortal world and unable to do harm. You can consign them to Oblivion."

Bob made a whistling sound.

What the hell? *How?* He doesn't have any *lips*.

"Ballsy," Bob admitted. "I mean, fighting a war like that...the more people you brought in to fight on your side, the more the information would spread, and the stronger a hold these demons would have. So you'd have to control who had the information. You'd have to lock that down *hard*."

"Very," I said. "I know that there are fewer than two hundred Venatori in the world. But we're organized in cells. I only know one other Venator."

"Venatori?" Bob said. "There's like five *thousand* of those dried-up old prunes. They've been helping the Council fight the war, remember?"

I waved a hand. "Those are the *Venatori Umbrorum*."

"Yeah," Bob said. "The Hunters of the Shadows."

"One way to translate their name," I said. "And it's the one they believe is correct. But it's more accurate to call them the Shadows of the Hunters. They don't know it, but we founded them. Gave them their store of knowledge. Use them to gather information, to help us keep an eye on things. And they're camouflage, too, to make our enemies have to work a little harder to find us."

"Enemies, right," Bob said. "A war has to have two sides."

I nodded. "Or more. There are a lot of...people...interested in the old demons. They're weak compared to what they once were, but they're still a route to power. Cults, priests, societies, individual lunatics. They're trying to keep the demons nailed to this world. We're trying to stop them." I shook my head. "The Oblivion War has been going on for more than five thousand years. Sometimes decades will pass without a single battle being fought. Sometimes it all goes insane."

"How many demons have you guys cut off?" Bob asked brightly. Then he chirped, "Oh, heh, I guess you wouldn't *know*, would you. If you kacked 'em, you don't even remember 'em."

"Yeah," I said.

"Kind of a thankless way to fight a war."

"Tell me about it," I said. "This is secret stuff, Bob. Just knowing it creates a kind of resonance in the mind. If someone knows to look for it, they can see it. If Harry finds out about the war, and anyone from either side realizes that he's aware..."

"The bad guys will assume that he's a Venator or a rival and kill him," Bob said, his manner suddenly sober. "And the Venatori will assume that he's a threat like the rest of the nutballs. They'll either consider him a security risk and kill him or impress him into joining their army. And he's already fighting one war."

"Yeah," I said.

"Um," Bob said. "One wonders why they won't do the same thing to me."

"You aren't mortal," I said. "Your knowledge won't bind anything to this world."

The skull somehow looked reassured. "That's true. Tell me about this client that's with my boss."

"You know about the Prosthanos Society?" I asked.

"Buncha lunatics in the Baltic region," Bob replied immediately. "They lop off their bits and pieces and replace them with grafts from inhuman sources. Demons and ghouls and such. Patchwork immortality."

I nodded. "The Stygian Sisterhood does the same thing—only with their psyches instead of with their physical bodies. They slice out the parts of their human personalities they don't want, and replace them pieces torn from inhuman minds."

"Cheery," Bob leered. "Sorority, huh? They hot?"

"It's generally advantageous," I said. "So for the most part, yes. They're dedicated to the service of a number of old demon-goddesses who they're trying to keep in the world through the publication of a book of rituals called the *Lexicon Malos*."

"So," the skull said. "Hot girl comes into Harry's office. He drools on her shoes, acts like an idiot, and doesn't take her up on her offer to do morally questionable things to him right then and there."

"Uh," I said. "I'm not sure if—"

"Being a stupid hero, he tells her not to worry, that he'll find her obvious sob-story decoy—I mean, lost child. Only when he does find the kid, he finds this book of rituals, too."

"And being a stalwart Warden of the White Council now..." I said.

Bob snorted. "He'll take them this book of dangerous rituals which anyone could use. And the Council will do with it what they did with the Necronomicon in order to defuse it."

I nodded. "They publish it, because they think that by making the rituals available to every nut who wants to try them, the power that comes out of them will be so diffused that it will never amount to any harm."

"Only the real danger isn't the rituals," Bob said. "But the knowledge of the beings behind them."

"And we might never be rid of them—just as we'll never be rid of the faeries."

Bob looked suddenly wistful. "You were trying to ditch the faeries?"

"The Venatori tried, yes," I said. "But the G-men stopped us cold."

"G-men? What, like the government?" Bob asked. "Like the Men in Black?"

"Like Gutenberg and the Grimms," I replied.

Bob narrowed his eyelights for a moment, apparently in thought. "This Stygian hottie. She laid a trap for you. She knew who you were, and what you'd do."

"I've crossed swords with the Sisterhood before. They know me." I shook my head. "I've got no idea why she messed up my face instead of killing me, though."

"Because Dresden would have sensed it," Bob said promptly.

"Eh?"

"Murdering someone with magic? It leaves an odor, and there isn't a body spray on earth that can hide it completely so soon after a kill. If Harry got close enough to sense a whiff of black magic on her, there wouldn't be any way she could pretend to be a damsel in distress."

"He'd still be able to tell she was a practitioner."

"Only if he actually touched her," Bob said. "And even then, if she's significantly different from a normal human, mentally, it'll alter the sense of her aura. Besides, sensing a little tingle of magical potential in a client is a whole lot different than realizing that she's spattered in supernatural gore."

"I get it. So instead she changed my face."

"Technically, she didn't *change* it," the skull said. "It's an illusion. You're still you under there. The question is why would she do *that*, particularly."

I frowned. "To slow me down," I said, thinking it through. It didn't take me long to figure out what the Stygian had in mind, and I clenched my teeth in frustration. "Oh, empty night. She's told Harry that there's a villain in the piece. She's shown him the picture of the bad man who took the poor kid." I gestured at my face. "And she's made *me* look like him."

"Damn," Bob said, admiration in his tone. "That's sneaky. Harry's awfully quick on the draw these days. If you mosey up, he might not give you a chance to explain anything."

I sighed. "The kind of day I'm having, he probably wouldn't. Are you going to help me or not?"

"Answer me one more question," the skull said, quieter now.

"Okay."

"Why?" he asked. "Why would vampires be a part of this? Why would something that eats people be interested in saving humanity from devouring demon gods?"

I snorted. "You want me to tell you that it's because in our secret hearts, we long to be heroes? Or that deep down, there's something in us that cries out for humanity, for redemption?" I shook my head and smiled at him, showing teeth. "At the end of the day? Because we don't like competition."

"Finally," Bob said, with a roll of his eyelights. "A motive I can *understand*. Okay."

"Okay?"

The skull turned on its shelf, to face the table. "I can show you how to find Harry. But the first thing we do is fix your face. Come on in, let me get a better look."

Mnemonic lightning flashed and boomed between my ears, and I felt myself smile. "No," I said.

The skull tilted slightly to one side, watching me. "No?"

"No. I've got a better idea."

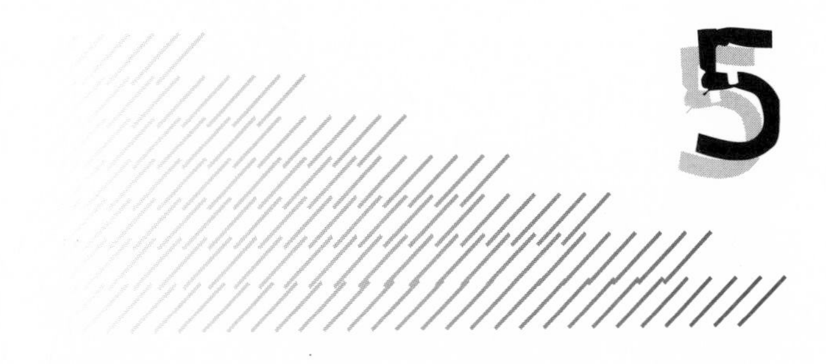

5

The skull tried to explain why the tracking spell he showed me was going to work when my own had failed, but about five seconds into the technical talk I started substituting "blah blah blah" for everything he was saying.

I'm not a wizard, okay? I'm a cheap hack. I don't care *why* it works, as long as it works.

The Stygian had staged her little charade in a warehouse down in Hammond. When I caught up to my brother, he and the Stygian were lurking in an alley across the street from the warehouse, watching the place. The Stygian was playing her part, that of the frightened, nervous female, anxious with the need to bring her offspring safely home again. She was a reasonably good actress, too, for someone with so little humanity. She was probably a couple of centuries old. She'd had time to get in some practice.

I went up the side of the building adjacent to the warehouse, so that I could get a look at the place, too. There were a couple more ghouls guarding the building, wearing the brown uniforms of private security personnel. They kept up a regular walking routine around the warehouse's exterior and interior, and they weren't bothering to so much as glance up at the rooftop I was on. It was five floors up with no fire escape and nothing but bricks to hold onto. Why should they?

I paced down to the back side of the warehouse, where Harry and the Stygian couldn't spot me, waited until the pacing ghouls were both out of sight, and then leapt the forty feet or so from my rooftop to the roof of the warehouse. I landed in a roll, in near complete silence, and froze for a long moment, waiting to see if anyone raised an outcry.

No one did. I hadn't been spotted.

I settled down to wait.

Harry made his move sometime between three and four in the morning, when the guards were most likely to be bored, tired, and convinced that nothing was going to happen tonight—and when there would be the fewest possible number of witnesses or innocent bystanders. From the front of the warehouse came his resonant baritone, crying out one of those pretend-Latin spell incantations he uses. There was a flash light, a boom like thunder, and a crash of something slamming into sheet metal with the force of a cannonball.

Scratch one ghoul. My brother hates the creatures with a passion so pure that it's almost holy. If his first attack hadn't killed the thing, he'd finish it off before long. I heard the other ghoul shriek as it began to transform.

Once everyone's attention was on the attack at the front door, I went in through a skylight.

The warehouse was stacked high with years of accumulated junk, consisting mostly of the remains of shipping crates, stacks of loading pallets, and broken boxes. An area in the center of the floor had been cleared, and the concrete had been heavily marked up with occult symbols painted in blood, around a table that was obviously intended to be an altar. A kid, a little boy maybe nine years old, was bound hand and foot on the table, his face blotchy from crying. He was screaming and struggling against the ropes, but was firmly secured to the table.

Harry cried out again. The glass in both windows at the front side of the warehouse exploded inward in a flash of scarlet light. Something that looked disturbingly like a severed arm went tumbling by the open doorway.

I kept looking until I spotted it—the *Lexicon Malos*, a leather-bound book, like a big old handwritten journal, just the kind of impressive grimoire occult nut-jobs like the Stygians are so giddy about. It rested on a little pedestal beside the table. It didn't actually have a flashing neon sign over it reading NOTICE ME, but it was pretty close.

I went hand over hand along the steel-beam rafters until I got to one of the girders that ran down the wall. Then I slid down it to the floor and hurried over to the altar and the pedestal. I opened the nylon backpack in my hands, stuffed the *Lexicon Malos* into it, zipped it closed, and then slid my arms through the shoulder straps.

I could have bailed, then. I suppose it would have been the smartest thing. Once the book was removed from the equation, the Stygian's entire operation was blown. Granted, she and the other members of the Sisterhood would try it again somewhere else, but they would have been stopped for the time being.

But the bitch had messed with my brother.

"For the time being" wasn't good enough.

Harry came through the front door of the warehouse, with the Stygian treading fearfully behind him, pretending to tremble. Tall, skinny, sharp-featured and somewhat rough-looking, Harry wore his usual wizarding gear—the black leather duster. He carried a carved staff in his left hand, a shorter, more heavily carved rod in his right, and the tip of the rod glowed with a sullen red-orange flame.

I was waiting for them.

I had wrapped the dark red blanket around my shoulders and upper body like some sort of dramatic ceremonial garb. I stood over the child, a wicked-looking knife I'd found lying on the altar in hand, with my head thrown back and a sneer on my illusion-covered face.

"So!" I boomed in my most overblown voice. "You have defeated my minions!"

"You have got to be kidding me," my brother said, staring at me with an expression somewhere between bemusement and naked contempt. "I mean…Jesus, look at this place. I've seen high school plays with a higher production value than this."

"Silence!" I thundered, pointing the knife at him. I only had eyes for the Stygian, in any case. She was staring at me with a look of blank surprise. Heh. Serves you right, sweetheart. You shouldn't make up stories about imaginary villains until you're certain that they won't come true. "Who dares interrupt my—"

"Yeah, you know what?" Harry asked. "*Forzare!*"

His staff snapped forward and an invisible truck hit me at thirty miles an hour.

I flew backwards, thirty feet or so, and hit a stack of loading pallets.

I went through them.

That hurt.

I hit the wall behind them.

I did not go through it.

That hurt even more.

I landed, dazed, and wobbled to my feet with the help of my demon. No problem, I told myself. I'd planned to fall back to this position in any case—just not quite that vigorously.

The circuit box for the building was on the wall two feet to my left. I reached out and killed the lights.

"Crouch down!" Harry shouted to the woman he thought he was protecting. "Stay still!"

My demon and I adjusted to the darkness almost instantly. The Stygian had done the same. She had produced a wavy-bladed dagger from nowhere, and was running toward me on silent feet, her eyes narrowed and intent.

I threw the prop knife I'd been holding when she was ten feet away. She slipped to one side, and it went spinning through the air, striking sparks off the far wall. Her knife struck at me, but I slammed the edge of one hand against her forearm, knocking it away before it could do more than scratch me. I followed that with a pair of sharp blows to the body, driving her back a step, and then drew my kukri from beneath the red blanket-robes, slashing at her head. I missed her, and the follow-up rake at her eyes that I made with my other hand failed to connect as well.

In the background, Harry had his priorities straight. He'd brought forth a little light from his amulet, and was cutting the child free from the makeshift altar. I felt my mouth stretch into a fierce grin.

"So smug," hissed the Stygian, her reptile-eyes flat. "But not for long." She raised her voice into a terrified scream. "Let me go! Don't touch me!"

Harry, holding the child over one shoulder in a fireman's carry, spun toward the sound, raising his blasting rod, and began hurrying toward me.

"Run, Venator," hissed the Stygian. "But the Blood of the Ancient Mothers is in your veins now. Enjoy your last hours."

The nick on my arm, the tiny cut from the dagger, suddenly felt very cold.

The book was out of Harry's hands. The child was safe.

I fled the building.

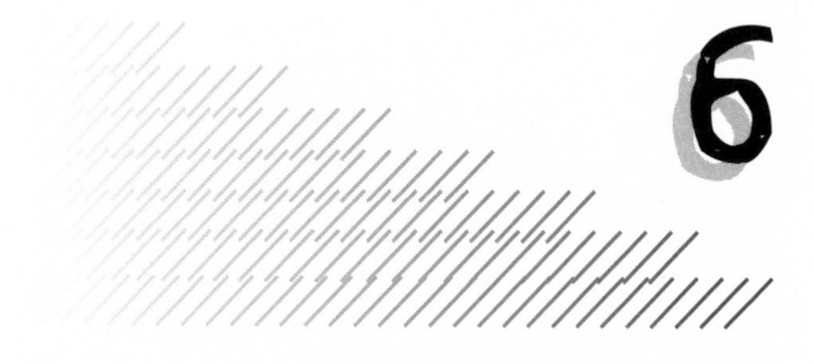

6

The wound was poisoned.

Without my demon, I don't think I would have lasted more than an hour. Even with its support, I was having trouble staying steady. The pain was horrible, and my whole body poured sweat even as I shivered with cold. The Hunger can usually overcome any kind of foreign substance—but while my demon might have been a powerful one, it was not well-fed, and I'd been using it hard all night. It had little strength left with which to fight the poison.

It was difficult, but I persevered for three hours.

That's how long it took for me to track the Stygian and catch her alone.

The sweep of my kukri had missed her head—but not the hairs growing out of it. And while my grasping fingers had not found her eyes an instant later, they had snatched those hairs out of the air before they could fall. The tracking spell the skull had taught me had been good enough to let me find the Stygian, despite any countermeasures she might have taken.

When she entered her hotel room, I was half an inch behind her. She never knew I was there until my lips touched the back of her neck, and I unleashed my demon upon her.

She let out a sudden gasp, as my Hunger, starved for so long, rushed into her flesh. Though she might have had the mind and thoughts of a dozen alien beings, she had a mortal life-force and a mortal body. A woman's body. And, as I had told the skull, a rather lovely one at that.

She tried to struggle for five or six seconds, until her nervous system succumbed to my Hunger, until the first orgasm ripped a moan of equal parts ecstasy, need, and despair from her throat.

"Shhhh," I told her, my teeth gently finding her earlobe, my hands roaming. "It won't hurt. I promise."

She cried out in despair again, as her body began moving in helpless acquiescence to desire, and my own reservations flickered and died before the raw, aching need of my Hunger.

I spend most of my life fighting my darker nature.

Most of it.

Not all of it.

I bore the Stygian to the floor and fed her to my demon.

Lara would help me get rid of the body.

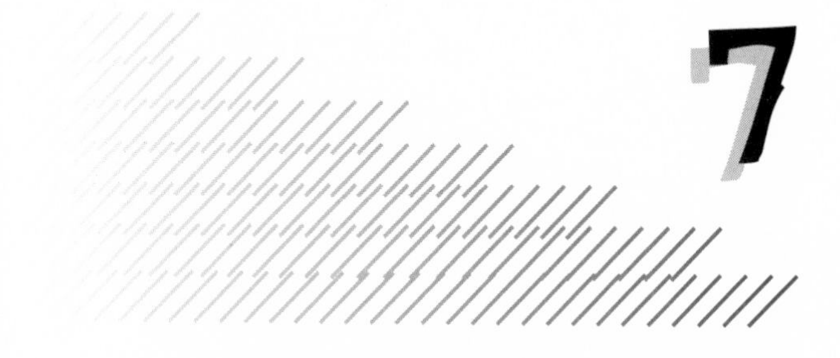

7

A long, long shower and the cleansing force of the rising sun had been enough to wash away the illusion that had obscured my true features.

I visited my brother at his office the next day.

"How's business?" I asked him.

He shook his head, scowling. "You know what? I've been doing so much gopher work for the Council and the Wardens, I think I must be forgetting how to be a private eye."

"Why's that?"

"Oh, I went up against this complete joke of a bad guy yesterday," he said. "Kidnapper. I mean, you should have seen this loser. He was a *joke*."

"Uh huh," I said.

"And somehow he manages to get away from me." Harry shook his head. "I mean, I got the kid back, no problem, but the little skeeve skated out on me."

"Maybe you're getting old."

He glowered at me. "The worst part is that the chick who hired me, it turns out, isn't even his mother. She was playing me all along. The kid's been missing for three days, and his *real* parents are trying to get the cops to freaking *arrest* me. After I pull him off of a freaking sacrificial alter—okay, a cheesy, stupid sacrificial alter, but a sacrificial alter all the same."

"Where's the chick?" I asked.

"Who knows?" Harry said, exasperated. "She's gone. Stiffed me, too. And good luck trying to get the kid's parents to pay me for the investigation and rescue. There's a better chance of electing a Libertarian president."

"The perils of the independent entrepreneur," I said. "You hungry?"

"You buying?"

"I'm buying."

He stood up. "I'm hungry." He put on his coat and walked with me toward the door, shaking his head. "I tell you, Thomas. Sometimes I feel completely unappreciated."

I found myself smiling.

"Wow," I said. "What's it like?"